The Cupcake Tree

written by R.L Cox

illustrated by Lauren Caster

Copyright 2016

All rights reserved

ISBN-13: 978-1519442147

ISBN-10: 151942149

Chrome Bunny LLC, North Bend, WA

A boy and girl walking down the street
looking for a tasty cupcake treat.

The smell of cupcakes excites your nose, leading you precisely where to go.

Around the corner on Cupcake Street is the baker who has these tasty treats.

"Where do cupcakes come from?" the little girl wants to know. "Why it's over the mountains and across the sea in a land only animals can see" replies the baker.

Starting as a crumb left by Mr. Squirrel in the fall, the cupcake tree grows to be three hundred feet tall!

Animals come from miles around to harvest and bring the cupcakes to the ground.

Buzz, Buzz, Buzz, hums Mr. Bee, "I'll carry the frosting to the cupcake tree." Up to the Lake of Frosting you fly, high on a mountain top oh so high.

Look overhead and what do you see?
Why it's a rainbow full of sprinkles for
the cupcake tree.

Up and down the tree, Mr. Squirrel runs as fast as can be down to Mr. Rabbit, who has a basket of cupcakes that can carry one, two or three.

Careful Mr. Rabbit as you run across the grass, Mr. Fox might not let you pass.

Watch out Mr. Rabbit!

Mr. Woodpecker seeing this horrible sight, takes flight to help Mr. Rabbits plight.

Run, run, run as fast as you can!

Mr. Owl with your feathers of white, where can you be tonight? Takes these cupcake treats on a moon lit flight.

Arriving at the baker's back door on Cupcake Street, Mr. Owl carefully sets down these tasty cupcake treats.

"A basket of tasty cupcakes oh what a surprise, I'll bring them into the bakery for a little boy and girls hungry eyes!"

"Now that you know the story of these tasty cupcake treats, which would you like to eat?"

Made in the USA
Lexington, KY
29 January 2016